Barbie ™

An Egg-stra Special Easter!

By Mary Man-Kong

Interior illustrated by Pamela Duarte, represented by Das Grüp, Inc.

A GOLDEN BOOK • NEW YORK

BARBIE and associated trademarks and trade dress are owned by, and used under license from, Mattel.
Copyright © 2014 Mattel. All Rights Reserved.
www.barbie.com
Published in the United States by Golden Books, an imprint of Random House Children's Books, a division of Random House LLC,
1745 Broadway, New York, NY 10019, and in Canada by Random House of Canada Limited, Toronto,
Penguin Random House Companies.
Golden Books, A Golden Book, and the G colophon are registered trademarks of Random House LLC.
ISBN 978-0-385-37319-7
randomhouse.com/kids
Book printed in the United States of America   10 9 8 7 6 5 4 3

Barbie loves Easter!

Barbie and Skipper decorate the living room
for their Easter party.

Connect the dots to see the shape of this cute balloon.

Stacie hangs the balloons for the Easter party.

Barbie decorates the room with beautiful flowers.

Time to color the Easter eggs!

Barbie and Chelsea create *egg*-cellent Easter eggs!

Create your own colorful Easter eggs.

Look up, down, backward, forward, and diagonally to find these Easter words:

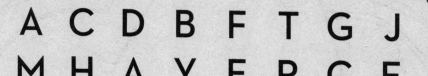

EASTER · BUNNY · EGGS · JELLY BEANS
CHOCOLATE · BASKETS · BONNET

```
A C D B F T G J
M H A Y E R C E
E O Y N N U B L
J C N K M L N L
P O S R B T Q Y
B L V U A Y P B
J A H Z S S M E
L T O X K G R A
V E T S E G T N
S E A S T E R S
I D S K S C P A
```

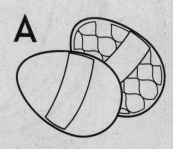

Stacie and Skipper love chocolate Easter bunnies!

"Bunnies are the best!" says Chelsea.

Chelsea and Skipper get baking!

Barbie and Stacie are great cupcake decorators.

Create your own cute Easter cupcake.

Barbie and Chelsea plant pretty flowers.

Barbie hides Easter eggs in the garden.

Blissa helps hide the eggs.

Barbie and Chelsea chase beautiful butterflies.

Can you find five differences between the top picture and the bottom one?

ANSWER: In the bottom picture, there is a cupcake missing on the top tier and on the bottom tier of the cupcake stand, there is a bunny sandwich missing, there is a lemon slice missing from the pitcher, and there is a different bow on one of the baskets.

Chelsea twirls in her pretty new Easter dress.

Draw yourself in your Easter dress.

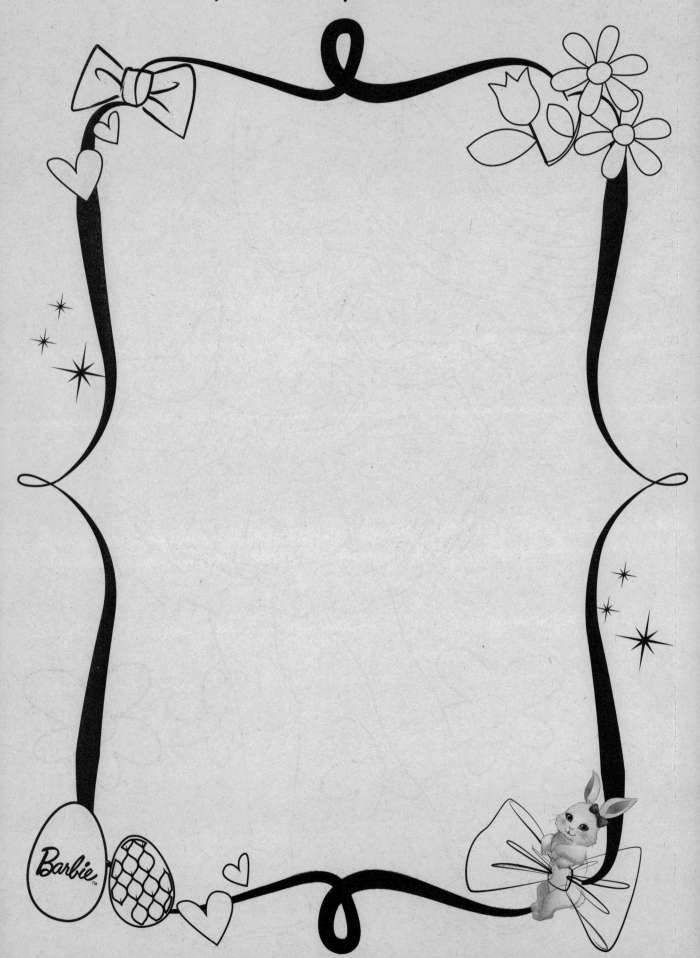

Some*bunny* is ready for the party!

Ding-dong! The guests are here!

Connect the dots to reveal Ken's present to Barbie.

For some*bunny* special!

Sequin and Blissa look *egg*-stra special.

Chelsea and Lacey lead the Easter parade.

Barbie and Skipper cheer!

Easter Egg Scramble
Unscramble these Easter words:

1

‾ ‾ ‾ ‾ ‾ ‾
E T B N N O

2

‾ ‾ ‾ ‾ ‾ ‾
S K A B T E

3

‾ ‾ ‾ ‾ ‾
U N B N Y

4

‾ ‾ ‾ ‾ ‾ ‾ ‾
W E L O F R S

5

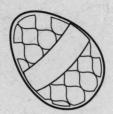

‾ ‾ ‾ ‾
G E G S

6

‾ ‾ ‾ ‾ ‾ ‾ ‾ ‾ ‾
S H C C O L A O T E

Barbie wears a beautiful bonnet.

Easter is for sharing.

Time for the Easter Egg Hunt!

How many Easter eggs can you find?

Connect the dots to show Barbie's pretty basket.

Stacie finds the golden Easter egg!

Everyone enjoys the Easter picnic.

Barbie has a surprise—baby chicks!

Use the code to find out what Easter game Barbie is playing.

A ♡   M ❀   O ◯
E ◯   G 🐰   R ✳
C 🎀   T 🌷   S ☆

Everyone plays Pin the Tail on the Bunny!

Barbie and her friends compete in the
Bunny Hop Race.

Skipper plays DJ.

Everyone does the Bunny Hop.

Stacie and Chelsea are off to the egg-roll race!

Help Chelsea get to the finish line.

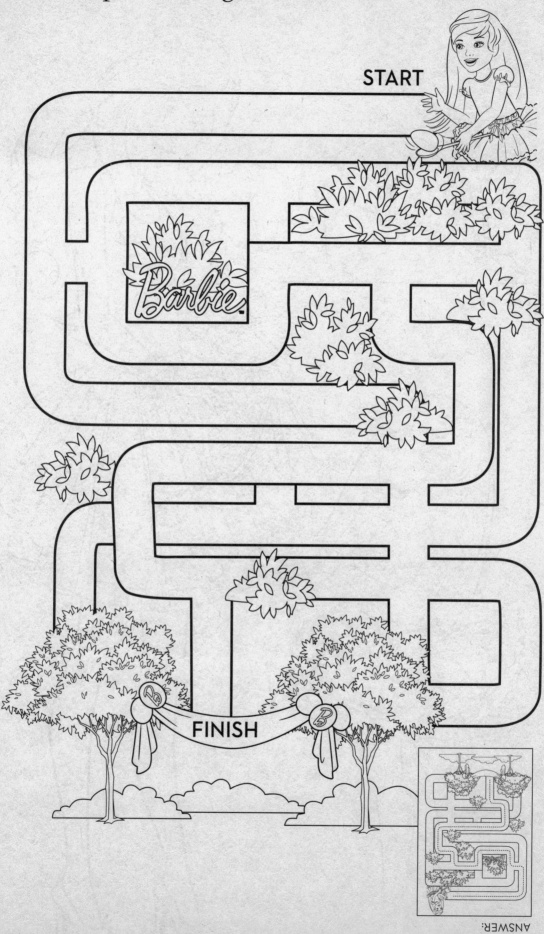

START

FINISH

ANSWER.

Chelsea wins first prize!

Everyone has an *egg*-stra special Easter!

Happy Easter!